For Mom & Dad, who are *always* the best parents. On every day!
—N.E. & L.E.

Dill & Bizzy: Opposite Day
Text copyright © 2017 by Nora Ericson
Illustrations copyright © 2017 by Lisa Ericson
All rights reserved. Manufactured in China.
No part of this book may be used or reproduced in any manner whatsoever without written permission except in the case of brief quotations
embodied in critical articles and reviews. For information address HarperCollins Children's Books, a division of
HarperCollins Publishers, 195 Broadway, New York, NY 10007.
www.harpercollinschildrens.com
Library of Congress Control Number: 2015958393
ISBN 978-0-06-230453-7

The artist used ink on paper colored digitally to create the illustrations for this book.
Typography by Dana Fritts
16 17 18 19 20 SCP 10 9 8 7 6 5 4 3 2 1
❖
First Edition

Dill & Bizzy
Opposite Day

By Nora Ericson   Illustrated by Lisa Ericson

HARPER
An Imprint of HarperCollinsPublishers

Dill was a duck. An odd duck.

BIZZY was a bird. A strange bird.

They were the best of friends.

Most days, Dill woke up early and Bizzy slept in late.

But one day
Bizzy woke up first . . .

and gave Dill a splashy surprise.

"It must be Opposite Day!" said Bizzy.

"All I know is that
usually I am dry,
but now I am wet," said Dill.
"Exactly," said Bizzy.
"Because it's Opposite Day!"

"Usually we start with breakfast,
so today we'll start with dinner!"
said Bizzy.

"Usually we go on a slow morning waddle, so today we'll go on a fast morning run!" said Bizzy.

"Wait up!" said Dill.

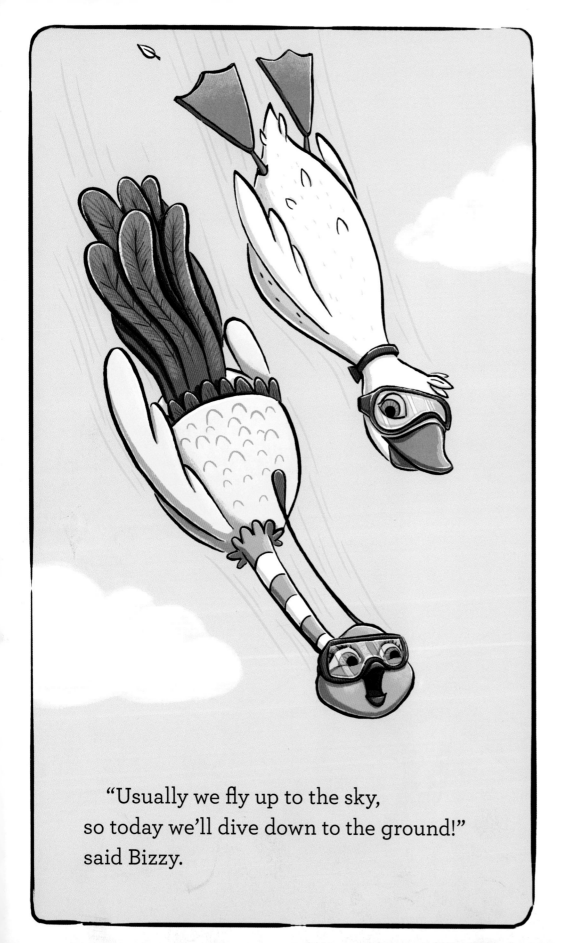

"Usually we fly up to the sky,
so today we'll dive down to the ground!"
said Bizzy.

"I don't think I like
Opposite Day!" said Dill.
"I just want a quiet rest."

"Oh, that means you love Opposite Day!" said Bizzy.
"And you want a loud dance party!"

"I don't want any more opposites!" said Dill.

"Aha! You want *lots more* opposites!" said Bizzy.

"You want to eat hot ice cream,

make your big feet small,

and turn your white feathers black!"

"I just want Opposite Day to be over," said Dill. "Let's go to bed so we can begin a new day tomorrow."

"Okay," said Bizzy.
"But instead of wearing
our pajama pants on our legs,
we'll put them on our heads.
And instead of washing
our faces, we'll get them dirty."

"Instead of reading a book and singing a song, we'll sing a book and read a song," said Bizzy. "And instead of saying good night, we'll say good morning."

"Good morning, Bizzy," said Dill.
"Good morning, Dill," said Bizzy. "Sour dreams!"

"But now we usually go to sleep!"
said Bizzy. "And the opposite of going
to sleep is staying up all night!
Opposite Day will go on forever!"

"We are doomed!" said Dill.

"At least we have each other," said Bizzy.

"But wait!" said Dill. "If it's truly Opposite Day, we can't be best friends!"

"Can't be best friends?" said Bizzy. "Ridiculous!"

"If it's truly Opposite Day,
we can't be friends at all!"
said Dill.

"Impossible!" said Bizzy.

"Bizzy, if it is *truly* Opposite Day,
we are worst enemies," whispered Dill.

"Never!" cried Bizzy. "Dill, we are *always* best friends! On every day!"

"Exactly," said Dill. "So it must not be Opposite Day after all."

"No, definitely not," said Bizzy.

They washed their faces,
read a book, and sang a song.
But they wore their pajama
pants on their heads again, just
for fun.

"Thank goodness for
best friends," said Bizzy.
"And perfectly normal days
together," said Dill.

"Good night, Dill," said Bizzy.
"Good night, Bizzy," said Dill.
"Sweet dreams."

"Ahh!" said Bizzy the next morning.
"It must be Backwards Day!!!"